For Helen, with love
~P.B.

For Tom and Emily
~M.B.

LITTLE TIGER PRESS
An imprint of Magi Publications
1 The Coda Centre, 189 Munster Road, London SW6 6AW
www.littletigerpress.com

First published in Great Britain 2005
This edition published 2009

Text copyright © Paul Bright 2005
Illustrations copyright © Matt Buckingham 2005

Paul Bright and Matt Buckingham have asserted their
rights to be identified as the author and illustrator of this
work under the Copyright, Designs and Patents Act, 1988

All rights reserved • ISBN 978-1-84506-881-3

Printed in China

10 9 8 7 6 5 4 3 2 1

Paul Bright   Matt Buckingham

Nobody Laughs
at a Lion!

Reading makes me smile!

Leap into a good book!

Let's have some fun!

LITTLE TIGER PRESS
London

In the cool of the morning, on
the edge of the jungle, the animals
were busy as can be.

They were running and racing,
climbing and clambering, crawling
and creeping all over the place.
Pa Lion sat and watched.

"You can see why I'm King of the
Jungle," he said. "It's because
I'm the best."

"Do stop boasting," said Ma Lion.
"And if you are the best, what are
you best at?"

Pa Lion thought for a while.

"Well, running for a start. You just watch."

Pa Lion bounded off through the long grass, sending the other animals scattering in fright.

As Pa Lion ran, the sleek, long-legged Cheetah raced past him with ease, and Cheetah laughed.

He laughed quietly, because
nobody laughs out loud at a lion.
But Pa Lion heard him.

"All right," said Pa Lion,
rather annoyed. "Cheetah
might be just a little bit
better at running. But I'm
best at . . . at climbing
trees. Look!"

Pa Lion dug his great claws into
the nearest tree and scrambled
and scratched and scrabbled, and
slowly heaved himself up on to the
lowest branch.

"Of course, some trees are more
difficult to climb than others,"
he said.

Monkey was swinging by his tail in the highest branches of the tree, and he saw Pa Lion climbing and he sniggered.

He sniggered quietly, because nobody sniggers out loud at a lion. But Pa Lion heard him.

"All right," said Pa Lion, grumpily.
"Monkey might be just a little bit better
   at climbing trees. But I'm the best at . . .
   at creeping through the long grass,
   quiet as quiet."

Pa Lion dropped into
a low crouch, then,
crawling and creeping,
slow as slow and quiet
as quiet, he moved
through the long grass.

Snake was slipping through the grass,
smooth and silent as a sigh. He saw Pa Lion
crawling and creeping, and he smiled. He
smiled to himself, because nobody smiles
at a lion. But Pa Lion saw him.

Pa Lion was beginning to feel angry.

"All right," he said. "Snake might be just a little bit better at creeping through the long grass, quiet as quiet. But I am the best at . . . at . . ."

"You are very good at sleeping," said Ma Lion.

"Sleeping doesn't count," said Pa Lion. Then he said, "I am the strongest. Watch me."

He pushed his great head against the trunk of a small tree, bending it until it broke with a loud crack!

Elephant was plodding past, leaving a trail of flattened bushes and broken trees in his path.

He saw Pa Lion and he lifted his trunk
and trumpeted. He trumpeted softly,
because not even an elephant trumpets
out loud at a lion. But Pa Lion heard him.

Now Pa Lion was furious. "All right,"
he said. "Maybe Elephant is just a
little bit stronger. But I am the best
at . . . the best at . . . Oh! I can't
think of anything!

"It really makes me want to . . .

AR

"... ROAR!"

And the sound of Pa Lion's
roar rolled and rumbled and
grew and grumbled and
echoed and thundered
through the jungle.

Pa Lion really *was* the very, very best at roaring.

Cheetah stopped laughing, and Monkey stopped sniggering, and Snake stopped smiling, and Elephant stopped trumpeting.

And Pa Lion was happy at last . . .
because NOBODY laughs at a lion!

Picture Dictionary

Look at the words below and put the correct
picture sticker next to each word.

lion   tree

cheetah   elephant

Did you put the stickers in the right place?
Then put a star on your reading tree!

Missing Words

Oh no! Lion has lost some of the words from the story! Can
you help him? Put the word stickers in the right spaces below.

smiles – creeping – grass – Snake – saw

_____ was slipping through the _____ ,

smooth and silent as a sigh. He saw Pa Lion crawling and

_____ , and he smiled. He smiled to himself, because

nobody _____ at a lion. But Pa Lion _____ him.

Did you get this right?
Add another star to your reading tree!

Crazy Commas

A **comma** is a mark that is used to separate words.
A comma sometimes tells the reader where to
pause in a sentence.
E.g. In the cool of the morning, on the edge of
the jungle, the animals were as busy as can be.

Put the **commas** into the sentences below.

1) They were running and racing climbing and
clambering crawling and creeping all over the place.

2) He pushed his great head against the trunk of a small
tree bending it until it broke with a loud crack!

3) Cheetah stopped laughing and Monkey stopped
sniggering and Snake stopped smiling and Elephant
stopped trumpeting.

 Did you find where the pauses should be?
Then add another star to your reading tree!

True or False

Pa Lion wants to be best at everything!
Which of these sentences is true and which is false?

	True	False
1) Pa Lion is better than Cheetah at running.	☐	☐
2) Pa Lion is better than Monkey at climbing.	☐	☐
3) Pa Lion is the very best at roaring.	☐	☐

 Did you get these right?
Add another star to your reading tree.

Wonderful Word Search

Find the following ten words in the word search below.
The words can be found written down and across.

clambering	tail	happy
trees	running	claws
nobody	strongest	slow
trunk		

O	B	R	T	R	E	E	S
C	U	U	Y	S	T	S	T
L	Z	N	G	S	A	W	R
A	P	N	D	L	E	M	O
M	W	I	M	O	N	I	N
B	K	N	A	W	B	T	G
E	O	G	L	S	R	Q	E
R	F	H	A	P	P	Y	S
I	C	L	A	W	S	V	T
N	O	B	O	D	Y	J	H
G	R	O	T	R	U	N	K
N	W	F	T	A	I	L	Y

 When you have done the word search,
add a star to your reading tree!

Amazing Alphabet

a b c d e f g h i j k l m n
o p q r s t u v w x y z

Put the word stickers in the right alphabetical order,
using the alphabet above to help.

roar – quiet – climb – grass – jungle

1) _____ 2) _____ 3) _____

4) _____ 5) _____

  Did you get this right? Remember to add
another star to your reading tree!

Same Meanings

Match the words on the left to the words on the right
with the same meaning. We've done the first one for you.

difficult   closest
sound   hard
angry   little
small   noise
nearest   furious

 Did you match the words?
Add another star to your reading tree.